A Guessing **ALPHABET**
of Feelings, Words, and Other Cool Stuff

A to Z

Do You Ever Feel Like Me?

text by **Bonnie Hausman**

photographs by **Sandi Fellman**

STYLING BY MEGAN KRIEMAN

DUTTON CHILDREN'S BOOKS · NEW YORK

zonked

zestful

zany

zealous

To my parents and Michael

● BH

To the two zany men in my life,
Charlie and Zander

● SF

A VERY BIG THANK-YOU to the children at the Little Red School House and
Elisabeth Irwin High School whose feelings, ideas, and hard work helped form this book;
and to their families for their time and endless support.

Thanks also to Randi Lestz, Boushelle Alvarez, Doug Keljikian, Natalie Bernstein, Judy
and Allen Glass, Jarett Glass, Tim Schneider, Cliff Nebel, and Suzanne Lander for their contri-
butions; and special thanks to Janet Pascal for creating the origami and a toy quilt.

We are also most grateful to Sara Reynolds and Donna Brooks for their creativity and
guidance.

We extend our sincere appreciation to all the New York City merchants who generously
donated merchandise for this book: Alphabets; A my name is...; Broadway Nut Shop; Chess
Forum; Dollhouse Antics; The Enchanted Forest®; Evolution; Fischer & Page; Fortunoff, the
source®; Gigi Accessories; Kidding Around; Leekan Designs; Les Tiny Doll House; Penny
Whistle Toys; West Side Kids; and Betty's Baubles (Philadelphia).

We gratefully acknowledge the following: Crayola® logo and serpentine design are reg-
istered trademarks of Binney & Smith, used with permission; Hanna Andersson, Portland,
Oregon, 1-800-222-0544, www.hannaandersson.com; LEGO and the LEGO logo are trademarks of The LEGO Group and are used here with special permission; Radio Flyer is a regis-
tered trademark of Radio Flyer Inc. of Chicago, Illinois. Used with permission.

CIP Data is available.
Published in the United States 1999 by Dutton Children's Books,
a division of Penguin Putnam Books for Young Readers
345 Hudson Street, New York, New York 10014
http://www.penguinputnam.com/yreaders/index.htm
Art direction and design by Sara Reynolds
Printed in Hong Kong
First Edition
ISBN 0-525-46216-3
1 2 3 4 5 6 7 8 9 10

CAN YOU GUESS

how the children in this book are feeling? Their faces and "stories" are clues. Think about how you would feel, and you will probably figure out how they are feeling.

● Here's a hint: The feelings in the book are arranged in alphabetical order from A to Z. The first feeling begins with A. The last one begins with Z. Look at the big letter on each page. The sound the letter makes will help you guess the feeling. The objects in the border all begin with that sound, too.

● Here's another hint: The word for the feeling is in the border. But watch out—there are other feeling words in the border, too!

● If you get stuck, just peek in the back of the book for the answer.

Good luck and have fun!

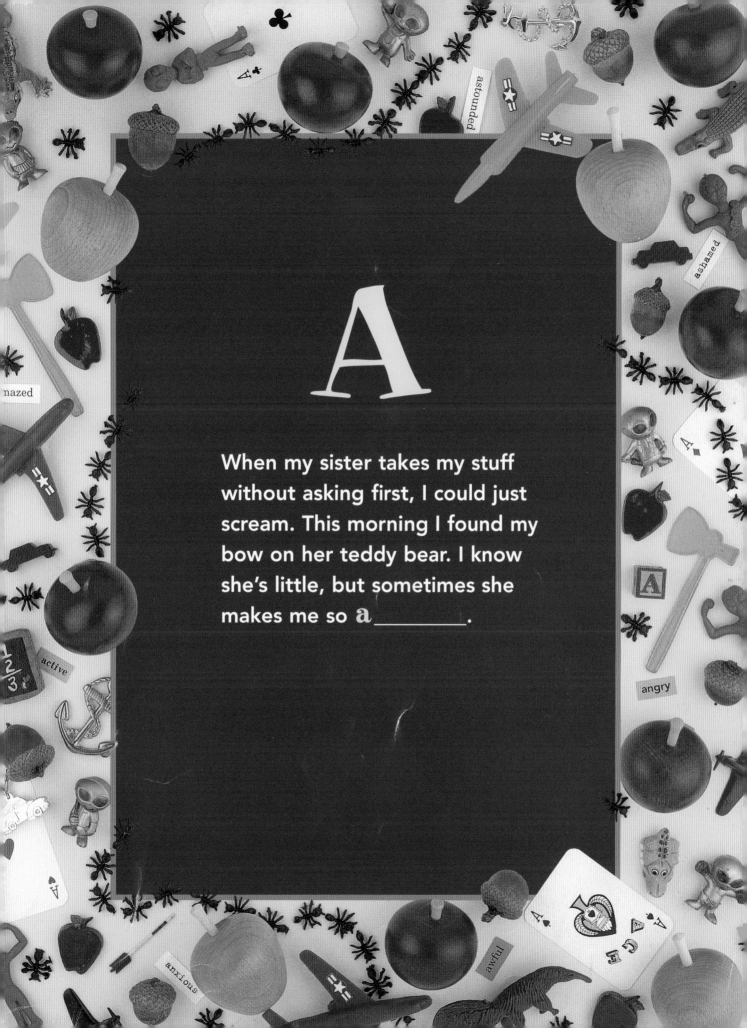

A

When my sister takes my stuff without asking first, I could just scream. This morning I found my bow on her teddy bear. I know she's little, but sometimes she makes me so a_____.

B

Today was the first day of school, and it was great. I felt so nervous this morning, I didn't want to go. I almost cried when I kissed my mom good-bye. But it all turned out okay because I was so b_____.

C

Huh? I don't understand what I'm supposed to do. My teacher spoke so fast that now I'm c_____.

D Guess what! I'm getting a puppy. I'm happier than happy. I'm d_____.

dangerous

distracted

different

disguised

delighted

disappointed

dizz

E

We were making a mural, and
I spilled the paint all over the
floor. Everyone laughed at me.
My teacher told me not to worry
and helped me clean it up. But
I wish I could disappear.
I feel so e_____.

embarrassed

energetic

excited

enthusiastic

eager

F We love playing together. We make up lots of neat games and make one another laugh and smile. We try not to leave anyone out. Other kids like to play with us because we're so f_____.

G Mine, mine, mine. I won't share these with anyone. Go ahead, call me g_____.

H

I'm going to my grandparents.
My clothes look snappy,
My eyes are twinkling,
I feel so h_____.

I

Oh, I can't stand it. That big hand is moving so slowly. As soon as school is over, I'm going on a play date. I just want to leave right now. Waiting makes me so i_____.

J They think they're so great, just because they have a new toy and won't let me play. I know they're just trying to make me

j_____.

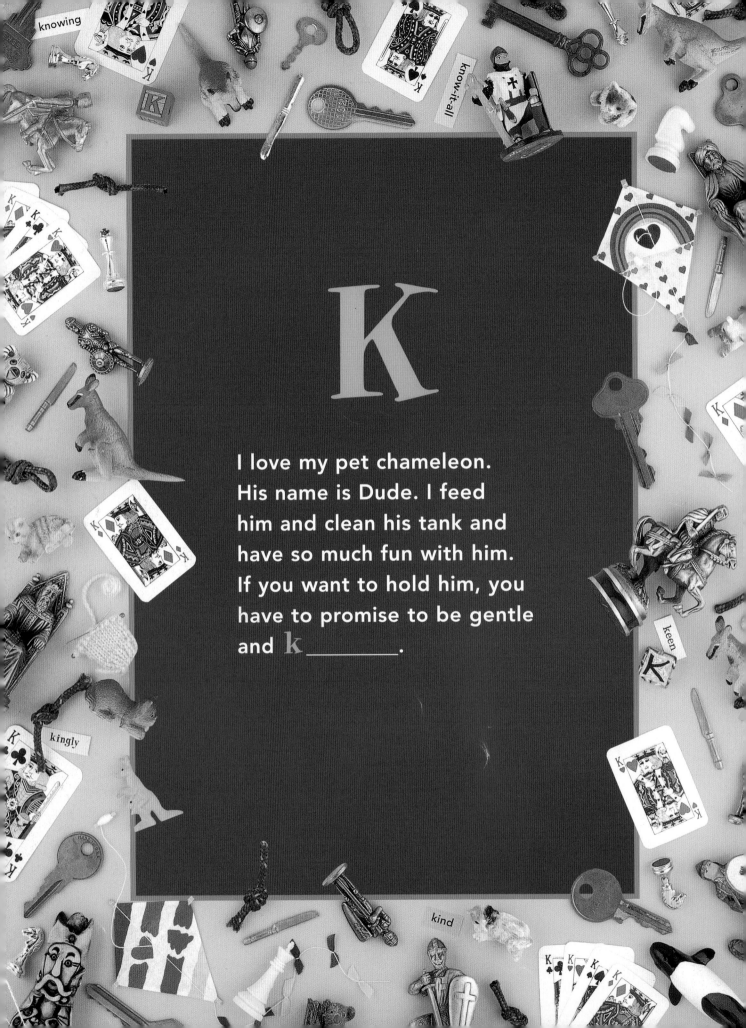

K

I love my pet chameleon. His name is Dude. I feed him and clean his tank and have so much fun with him. If you want to hold him, you have to promise to be gentle and k_____.

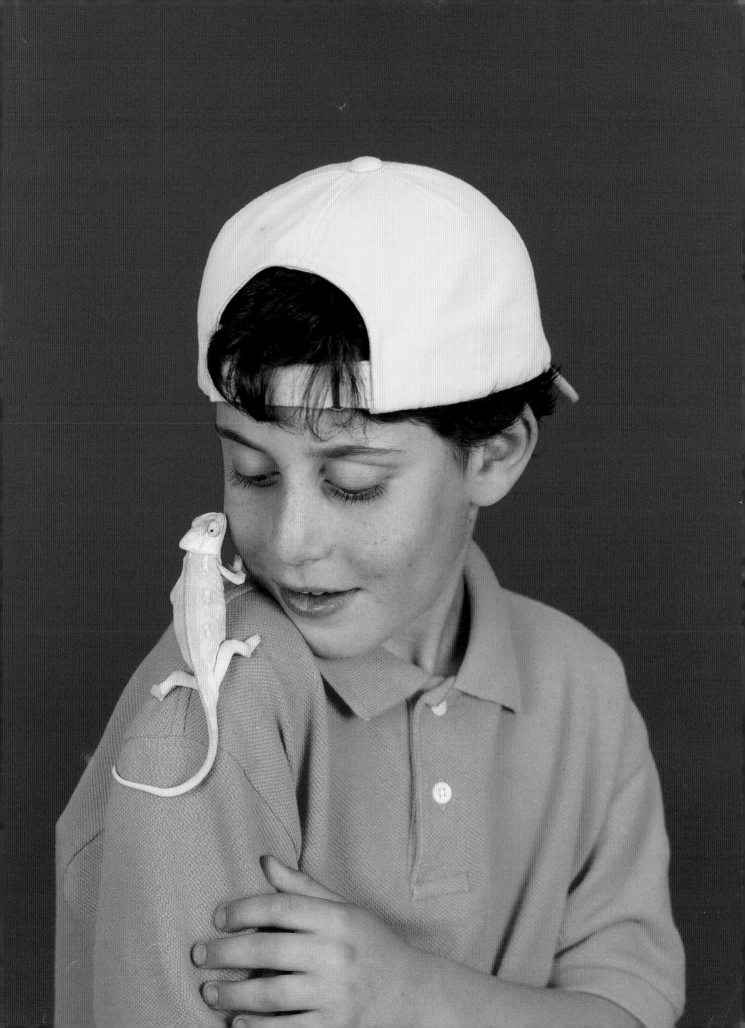

L

We just moved into a new house. I miss all of my old friends. My dad says that I'll make new friends soon. I hope he's right. I don't like feeling l_____.

loopy

loving

M

Uh-oh.
If my mom catches me playing with her makeup again, I'm going to be in big trouble. But I just can't help being a little m _____.

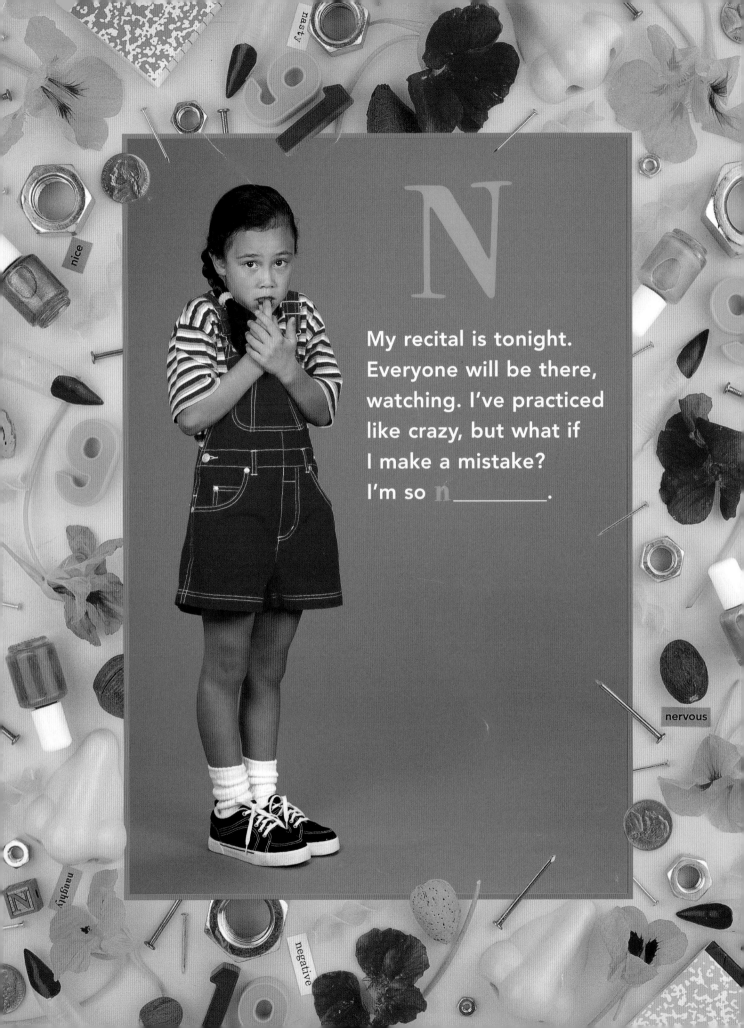

N

My recital is tonight. Everyone will be there, watching. I've practiced like crazy, but what if I make a mistake? I'm so n_____.

O Help! I promised to clean my room before my cousins came over. But I forgot. There's stuff everywhere, and they'll be here in fifteen minutes. I don't know where to start. I'm **O_____**.

original
overwhelmed
obstinate
open-minded
One Way
observant
optimistic
okay
outraged

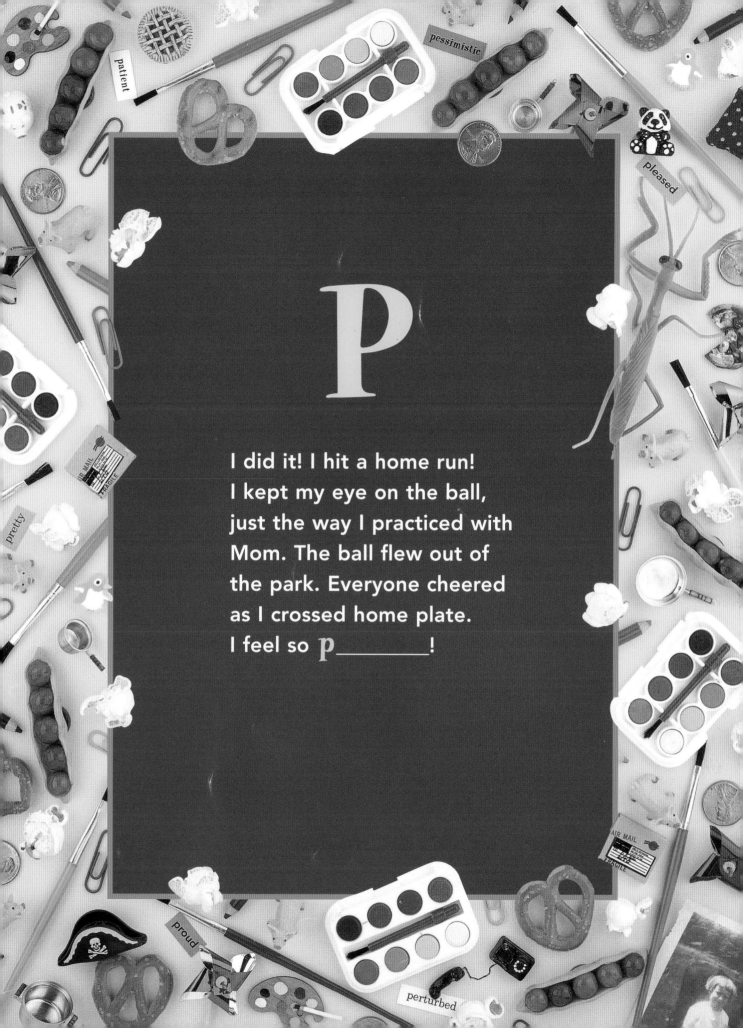

P

I did it! I hit a home run!
I kept my eye on the ball,
just the way I practiced with
Mom. The ball flew out of
the park. Everyone cheered
as I crossed home plate.
I feel so p_____!

patient

pessimistic

pleased

pretty

proud

perturbed

Q At the party I ate a hamburger, a slice of pizza, chips, carrots, two pieces of cake with ice cream on top, and all the candy in my party bag. It went down easy. But now my stomach hurts. I feel q_____.

quinky

queasy

R Our teacher says there's not a calm one amongst us when we're out of control and acting r_____.

S

I went into the haunted house
Because I was dared.
But it was too dark and spooky,
And now I'm s_____.

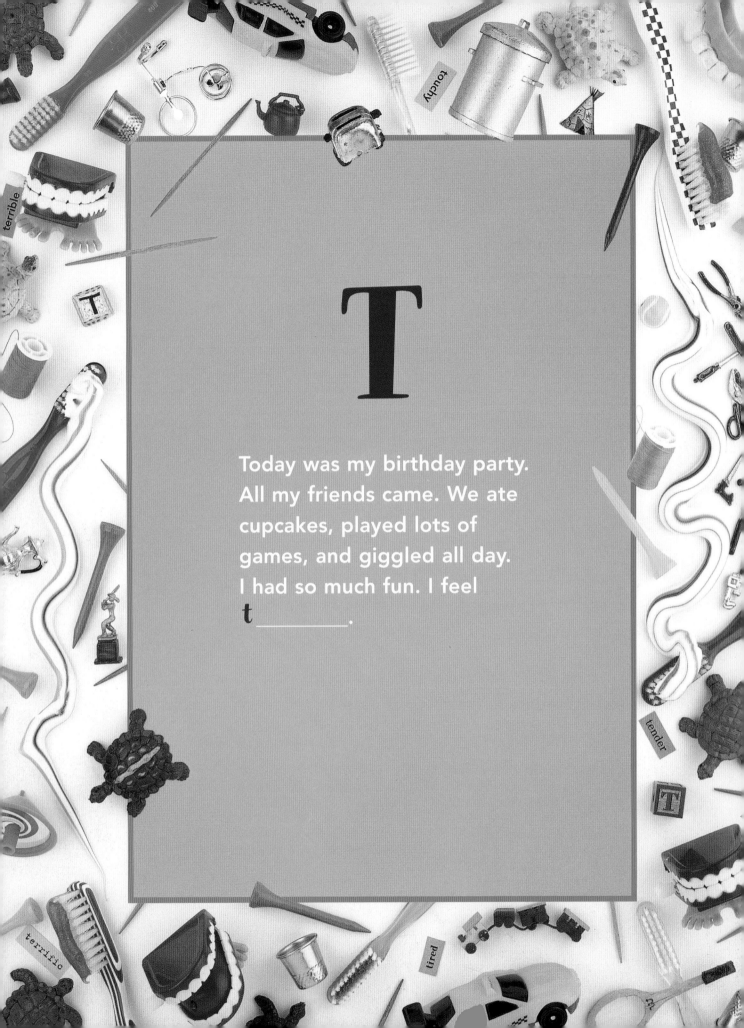

T

Today was my birthday party. All my friends came. We ate cupcakes, played lots of games, and giggled all day. I had so much fun. I feel t_____.

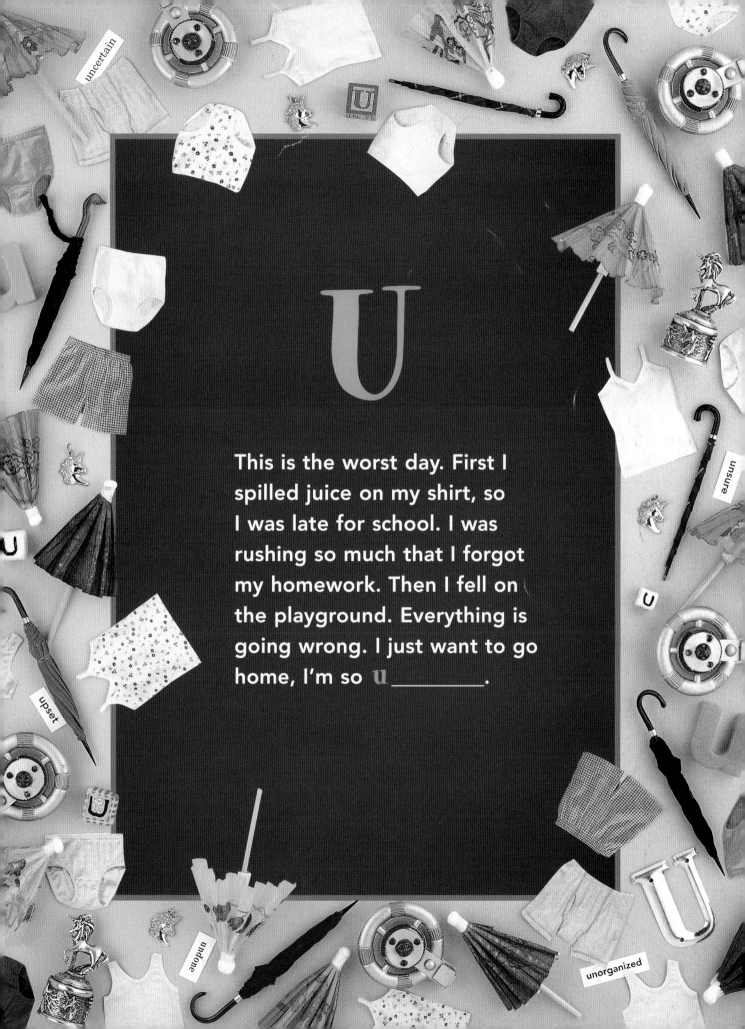

U

This is the worst day. First I spilled juice on my shirt, so I was late for school. I was rushing so much that I forgot my homework. Then I fell on the playground. Everything is going wrong. I just want to go home, I'm so u_____.

uncertain

unsure

upset

undone

unorganized

V Sometimes I think I could stare at myself in the mirror all day. I like how I look with my headband and nail polish. Does that make me **V**_____?

W

I have to go to the doctor. What if she gives me a shot? That can really hurt. I know because I had one last time. I'm so W_____.

X

What a tiring day. We went to the zoo and walked and walked. Then we went to soccer practice and ran and ran. We're e**X**_____.

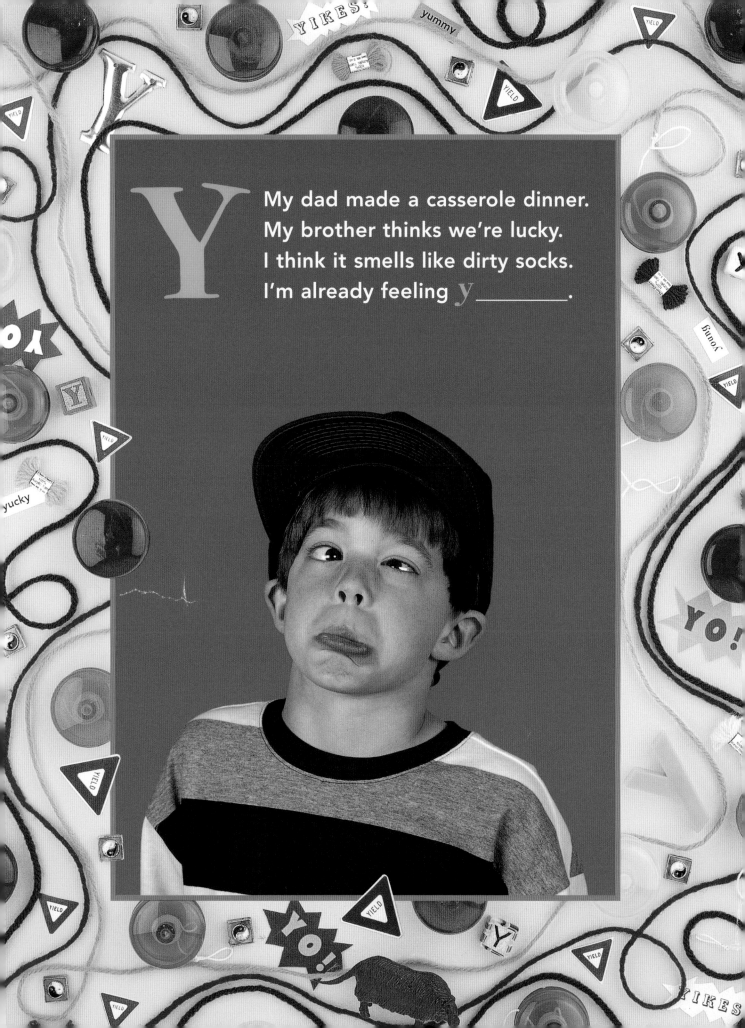

Y

My dad made a casserole dinner.
My brother thinks we're lucky.
I think it smells like dirty socks.
I'm already feeling y_____.

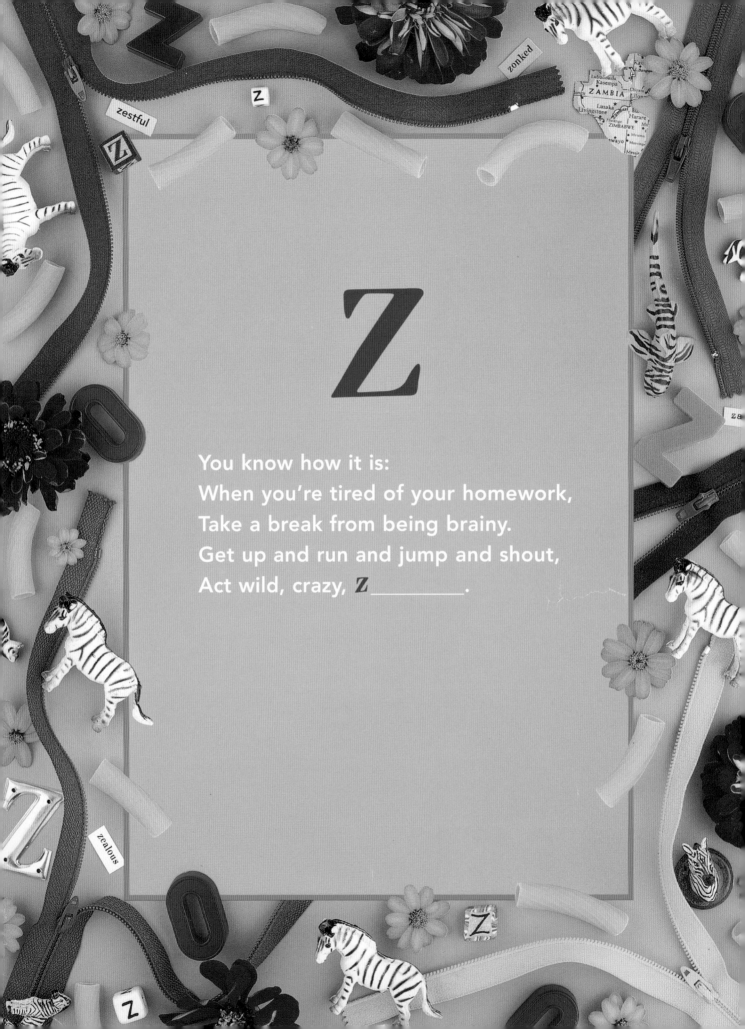

Z

You know how it is:
When you're tired of your homework,
Take a break from being brainy.
Get up and run and jump and shout,
Act wild, crazy, Z_____.

angry • BORDER OBJECTS: "A" block aces acorns addition airplanes aliens alligators anchors anteater (also called "aardvark") ants apples arrow automobiles axes • WORDS: active amazed angry anxious ashamed astounded awful

brave • BORDER OBJECTS: "B" block babies baby bottles backgammon set balloon barrettes baseball bat baseballs basket bats beads bear beetles belt binoculars birds birthday cake bone boots bow bowling pins broom bubble gum bucket buffalo butterflies buttons • WORDS: bashful beautiful bedazzled blue bored brave

confused • BORDER OBJECTS: "C" blocks cake calculator camera candle candy candy canes candy corn cat caterpillar centipede chair cheese chess set clock clothespins clowns coffee coins compass cows crayons cricket crutches • WORDS: calm clever confident confused cool crazy curious

delighted • BORDER OBJECTS: "D" blocks daisies dalmatians dartboard darts diamond ring diamonds dice dimes dinosaurs dogs dolls dolphin dragonflies dresses duck dumbbells • WORDS: dangerous delighted different disappointed disguised distracted dizzy

embarrassed • BORDER OBJECTS: "E" blocks eagles earrings Easter eggs eel eggplants eggs eights elephants eleven envelopes erasers eyeballs eyelashes • WORDS: eager embarrassed energetic enthusiastic excited

friendly • BORDER OBJECTS: "F" blocks fans fawn feathers feet fingers fish flags flamingos flies flipper football forks fossils frogs • WORDS: fidgety focused friendly frightened frustrated funny furious

greedy • BORDER OBJECTS: "G" block gecko geodes gifts gingerbread house giraffe globes goldfish golf club gorillas grass grasshoppers guitar gum gumdrops • WORDS: generous glad good greedy gross guilty

happy • BORDER OBJECTS: "H" blocks hair dryer hammer hands hangers hats heart milagro hearts hedgehog helicopter hippopotamuses hockey stick horses hose hot dogs hourglass hula dancers • WORDS: happy hopeful horrible hurt hyper

impatient • BORDER OBJECTS: "I" blocks ice cream ice-cream cones ice-cream sandwich ice-cream sundae ice cubes ice skates Idaho Illinois inches Indiana Iowa insects ivy • WORDS: ill impatient incredible innocent insecure irritable itchy

jealous • BORDER OBJECTS: "J" blocks jacket jack-in-the-boxes jack-o'-lanterns jacks jelly jellybeans jets jewelry jewels jokers • WORDS: jealous jittery joyful jumpy

kind • BORDER OBJECTS: "K" blocks kangaroos keys killer whale kings kites kittens knights knitting knives knots koalas • WORDS: keen kind kingly knowing know-it-all

lonely • BORDER OBJECTS: ladles ladybugs lamps Lego blocks lemon drops licorice lighthouse lima beans lions lips lipsticks little red schoolhouse lizard llama lobster locks lollipops • WORDS: lonely loopy loving lucky

mischievous • BORDER OBJECTS: "M" blocks macaroni marbles matches mazes mice mitt money monkeys monster moons moose mop mustache • WORDS: mad magnificent marvelous mischievous miserable mixed-up moody mopey musical

nervous • BORDER OBJECTS: "N" block nail polish nails nasturtiums nickels nine nineteen ninety-one noodles noses notebooks nuts • WORDS: nasty naughty negative nervous nice

overwhelmed • BORDER OBJECTS: "O" block oar octopi one-way sign orange jelly slices oranges origami owls • WORDS: observant obstinate okay open-minded optimistic original outraged overwhelmed

proud • BORDER OBJECTS: packages paintbrushes paints panda bear pans paper clips pea pods pencils penguins pennies phone photograph pie piggy bank pigs pillow pinwheels pirate hat pizza popcorn pots praying mantis pretzels • WORDS: patient perturbed pessimistic pleased pretty proud

queasy • BORDER OBJECTS: "Q" blocks quarters quartz Quebec queens question marks quills quilt quotation marks • WORDS: quarrelsome queasy questionable quiet quirky

rambunctious • BORDER OBJECTS: rabbits raccoon race cars radishes ram rat rattles reindeer rhinoceroses ribbons rings robot rocking horses rocks rubber bands rugs • WORDS: radiant rambunctious responsible rested rotten

scared • BORDER OBJECTS: "S" block sailboat saw scales scissors sea horses shells shoes shovel skateboard skeletons skis skunk sled snakes spools spoons stamps starfish stars Statue of Liberty strawberries sunflowers sushi • WORDS: sad scared selfish sensitive silly stubborn sweet

terrific • BORDER OBJECTS: "T" blocks taxicabs teapots tees teeth tennis ball tennis racket tepee thimbles thread toaster tools tooth brushes tooth picks toothpaste top train trash can tricycle trophy turtles • WORDS: tender terrible terrific tired touchy

upset • BORDER OBJECTS: "U" blocks UFOs umbrellas undershirts underpants unicorns • WORDS: uncertain undone unorganized unsure upset

vain • BORDER OBJECTS: "V" blocks vacuum cleaners valentines vases vegetables vest Victrola violets violins vitamins volleyball • WORDS: vain vengeful vibrant vicious vivacious vulnerable

worried • BORDER OBJECTS: "W" blocks waffles wagon wheels wagons watch watering cans watermelons well wheels whistles wigs wing nuts witch words worms wrenches • WORDS: wacky weak wiggly wired worried

 eXhausted • BORDER OBJECTS: "X" blocks eXclamation points eXit signs x-larges Xmas trees X rays xylophones xylophone sticks • WORDS: eXcellent eXcited eXhausted eXhilarated eXtraordinary eXtravagant

 yucky • BORDER OBJECTS: "Y" blocks yak yarn yield signs yikes yin/yangs yo yo-yos • WORDS: young yucky yummy

 zany • BORDER OBJECTS: "Z" blocks Zambia zebras zeros zinnias zippers ziti • WORDS: zany zealous zestful zonked

How This Book Began

Learning to read is a challenging task. In my classroom, we begin by studying the alphabet and the sounds each letter makes. One of the projects we work on is a three-dimensional alphabet to hang on our classroom wall. We cut large letters out of cardboard and cover them with colorful construction paper. The children bring in objects from home that begin with the sound of the letter we're studying. Then we glue each item to the letter, and within weeks, our alphabet is complete. One year, a parent who is a professional photographer heard me comment that I had always wanted to photograph the letters to create an alphabet book. She said, "Let's do it!" And we did.

To enhance our study, we decided to link learning letters with exploring feelings, since an important part of our curriculum includes helping children understand what they are feeling and how to communicate that effectively. Discussions about feelings come up every day in first grade. This particular class of first-graders felt certain that you can be a better friend if you can figure out how other people are feeling.

At her studio, Sandi Fellman explained to the children what a photographer does and demonstrated how a camera works. Wearing their letters, the children portrayed the feelings they had chosen and took Polaroids of one another. The results were terrific—each child's expression truly captured the feeling. We color-copied the Polaroids and created the "Spectacular Alphabet Book." Our homemade book intrigued a parent who is an art director at a children's book publisher. She thought children across the country would enjoy the different aspects of the book and all the "stuff" that went with the letters. So we put our adult talents together with the children's joy and ingenuity to create the book you see here.

BONNIE HAUSMAN